The Beautiful People

The Beautiful People

CHARLES BEAUMONT

ÆGYPAN PRESS

Special thanks to Greg Weeks, Dianna Adair, and the Online
Distributed Proofreading Team (which can be found at
http://www.pgdp.net).

This story originlly appeared in the September 1952 issue of
If Worlds of Science Fiction.

The Beautiful People
A publication of
ÆGYPAN PRESS

www.aegypan.com

Mary was a misfit. She didn't want to be beautiful. And she wasted time doing mad things — like eating and sleeping.

Mary sat quietly and watched the handsome man's legs blown off; watched further as the great ship began to crumple and break into small pieces in the middle of the blazing night. She fidgeted slightly as the men and the parts of the men came floating dreamily through the wreckage out into the awful silence. And when the meteorite shower came upon the men, gouging holes through everything, tearing flesh and ripping bones, Mary closed her eyes.

"Mother."

Mrs. Cuberle glanced up from her magazine.

"Hmm?"

"Do we have to wait much longer?"

"I don't think so. Why?"

Mary said nothing but looked at the moving wall.

"Oh, that." Mrs. Cuberle laughed and shook her head. "That tired old thing. Read a magazine, Mary, like I'm doing. We've all seen *that* a million times."

"Does it have to be on, Mother?"

"Well, nobody seems to be watching. I don't think the doctor would mind if I switched it off."

Mrs. Cuberle rose from the couch and walked to the wall. She depressed a little button and the life went from the wall, flickering and glowing.

Mary opened her eyes.

"Honestly," Mrs. Cuberle said to a woman sitting beside her, "you'd think they'd try to get something else. We might as well go to the museum and watch the first landing on Mars. The Mayoraka Disaster — really!"

The woman replied without distracting her eyes from the magazine page. "It's the doctor's idea. Psychological."

Mrs. Cuberle opened her mouth and moved her head up and down knowingly.

"Ohhh. I should have known there was *some* reason. Still, who watches it?"

"The children do. Makes them think, makes them grateful or something."

"Ohhh."

"Psychological."

Mary picked up a magazine and leafed through the pages. All photographs, of women and men. Women like Mother and like the others in the room; slender, tanned, shapely, beautiful women; and men with large muscles and shiny hair. Women and men, all looking alike, all perfect and beautiful. She folded the magazine and wondered how to answer the questions that would be asked.

"Mother —"

"Gracious, what is it now! Can't you sit still for a minute?"

"But we've been here three hours."

Mrs. Cuberle sniffed.

"Do — do I really have to?"

"Now don't be silly, Mary. After those terrible things you told me, of *course* you do."

An olive-skinned woman in a transparent white uniform came into the reception room.

"Cuberle. Mrs. Zena Cuberle?"

"Yes."

"Doctor will see you now."

Mrs. Cuberle took Mary's hand and they walked behind the nurse down a long corridor.

A man who seemed in his middle twenties looked up from a desk. He smiled and gestured toward two adjoining chairs.

"Well — well."

"Doctor Hortel, I —"

*T*he doctor snapped his fingers.

"Of course, I know. Your daughter. Ha ha, I certainly do know your trouble. Get so many of them nowadays — takes up most of my time."

"You do?" asked Mrs. Cuberle. "Frankly, it had begun to upset me."

"Upset? Hmm. Not good. Not good at all. Ah, but then — if people did not get upset, we psychiatrists would be out of a job, eh? Go the way of the early M. D. But, I assure you, I need hear no more." He turned his handsome face to Mary. "Little girl, how old are you?"

"Eighteen, sir."

"Oh, a real bit of impatience. It's just about time, of course. What might your name be?"

"Mary."

"Charming! And so unusual. Well now, Mary, may I say that I understand your problem — understand it thoroughly?"

Mrs. Cuberle smiled and smoothed the sequins on her blouse.

"Madam, you have no idea how many there are these days. Sometimes it preys on their minds so that it affects them physically, even mentally. Makes them act strange, say peculiar, unexpected things. One little girl I recall was so distraught she did nothing but brood all day long. Can you imagine!"

"That's what Mary does. When she finally told me, doctor, I thought she had gone — *you* know."

"That bad, eh? Afraid we'll have to start a re-education program, very soon, or they'll all be like this. I believe I'll suggest it to the senator day after tomorrow."

"I don't quite understand, doctor."

"Simply, Mrs. Cuberle, that the children have got to be thoroughly instructed. Thoroughly. Too much is taken for granted and childish minds somehow refuse to accept things without definite reason. Children have become far too intellectual, which, as I trust I needn't remind you, is a dangerous thing."

"Yes, but what has this to do with —"

"With Mary? Everything, of course. Mary, like half the sixteen, seventeen and eighteen year olds today, has begun to feel acutely self-conscious. She feels that her body has developed sufficiently for the Transformation — which of course it has not, not quite yet — and she cannot understand the complex reasons that compel her to wait until some future date. Mary looks at you, at the women all about her, at the pictures, and then she looks into a mirror. From pure perfection of body, face, limbs, pigmentation, carriage, stance, from simon-pure perfection, if I may be allowed the expression, she sees herself and is horrified. Isn't that so, my dear child? Of course — of course. She asks herself, why must I be hideous, unbalanced, oversize, undersize, full of revolting skin eruptions, badly schemed organically? In short, Mary is tired of being a monster and is overly anxious to achieve what almost everyone else has already achieved."

"But —" said Mrs. Cuberle.

"This much you understand, doubtless. Now, Mary, what you object to is that our society offers you, and the others like you, no convincing logic on the side of waiting until age nineteen. It is all taken for granted, and you want to know why! It is that simple. A non-technical explanation will not suffice — mercy no! The modern child wants facts, solid technical data, to satisfy her every question. And that, as you can both see, will take a good deal of reorganizing."

"But —" said Mary.

"The child is upset, nervous, tense; she acts strange, peculiar, odd, worries you and makes herself ill because it is beyond our meager powers to put it across. I tell you, what we need is a whole new basis for learning. And, that will take doing. It will take *doing*, Mrs. Cuberle. Now, don't you worry about Mary, and don't *you* worry, child. I'll prescribe some pills and —"

"No, no, doctor! You're all mixed up," cried Mrs. Cuberle.

"I beg your pardon, Madam?"

"What I mean is, you've got it wrong. Tell him, Mary, tell the doctor what you told me."

Mary shifted uneasily in the chair.

"It's that — I don't want it."

The doctor's well-proportioned jaw dropped.

"Would you please repeat that?"

"I said, I don't want the Transformation."

"D — Don't want it?"

"You see? She told me. That's why I came to you."

The doctor looked at Mary suspiciously.

"But that's impossible! I have never heard of such a thing. Little girl, you are playing a joke!"

Mary nodded negatively.

"See, doctor. What can it be?" Mrs. Cuberle rose and began to pace.

*T*he doctor clucked his tongue and took from a small cupboard a black box covered with buttons and dials and wire.

"Oh no, you don't think — I mean, could it?"

"We shall soon see." The doctor revolved a number of dials and studied the single bulb in the center of the box. It did not flicker. He removed handles from Mary's head.

"Dear me," the doctor said, "dear me. Your daughter is perfectly sane, Mrs. Cuberle."

"Well, then what is it?"

"Perhaps she is lying. We haven't completely eliminated that factor as yet; it slips into certain organisms."

More tests. More machines and more negative results.

Mary pushed her foot in a circle on the floor. When the doctor put his hands to her shoulders, she looked up pleasantly.

"Little girl," said the handsome man, "do you actually mean to tell us that you *prefer* that body?"

"Yes sir."

"May I ask why."

"I like it. It's — hard to explain, but it's me and that's what I like. Not the looks, maybe, but the *me.*"

"You can look in the mirror and see yourself, then look at — well, at your mother and be content?"

"Yes, sir." Mary thought of her reasons; fuzzy, vague, but very definitely there. Maybe she had said the reason. No. Only a part of it.

"Mrs. Cuberle," the doctor said, "I suggest that your husband have a long talk with Mary."

"My husband is dead. That affair near Ganymede, I believe. Something like that."

"Oh, splendid. Rocket man, eh? Very interesting organisms. Something always seems to happen to rocket men, in one way or another. But — I suppose we should do something." The doctor scratched his jaw. "When did she first start talking this way," he asked.

"Oh, for quite some time. I used to think it was because she was such a baby. But lately, the time getting so close and all, I thought I'd better see you."

"Of course, yes, very wise. Er — does she also do odd things?"

"Well, I found her on the second level one night. She was lying on the floor and when I asked her what she was doing, she said she was trying to sleep."

Mary flinched. She was sorry, in a way, that Mother had found that out.

"To — did you say 'sleep'?"

"That's right."

"Now where could she have picked that up?"

"No idea."

"Mary, don't you know that nobody sleeps anymore? That we have an infinitely greater life-span than our poor ancestors now that the wasteful state of unconsciousness has been conquered? Child, have you actually *slept*? No one knows how anymore."

"No sir, but I almost did."

The doctor sighed. "But, it's unheard of! How could you begin to try to do something people have forgotten entirely about?"

"The way it was described in the book, it sounded nice, that's all." Mary was feeling very uncomfortable now. Home and no talking man in a foolish white gown. . . .

"Book, book? Are there *books* at your Unit, Madam?"

"There could be — I haven't cleaned up in a while."

"That is certainly peculiar. I haven't seen a book for years. Not since '17."

Mary began to fidget and stare nervously about.

"But with the tapes, why should you try and read books — where did you get them?"

"Daddy did. He got them from his father and so did Grandpa. He said they're better than the tapes and he was right."

Mrs. Cuberle flushed.

"My husband was a little strange, Doctor Hortel. He kept those things despite everything I said.

"Dear me, I — excuse me."

The muscular, black-haired doctor walked to another cabinet and selected from the shelf a bottle. From the bottle he took two large pills and swallowed them.

"Sleep — books — doesn't want the Transformation — Mrs. Cuberle, my *dear* good woman, this is grave. Doesn't want the Transformation. I would appreciate it if you would change psychiatrists: I am very busy and, uh, this is somewhat specialized. I suggest Centraldome. Many fine doctors there. Good-bye."

The doctor turned and sat down in a large chair and folded his hands. Mary watched him and wondered why the simple statements should have so changed things. But the doctor did not move from the chair.

"Well!" said Mrs. Cuberle and walked quickly from the room.

The man's legs were being blown off again as they left the reception room.

Mary considered the reflection in the mirrored wall. She sat on the floor and looked at different angles of herself: profile, full-face, full length, naked, clothed.

Then she took up the magazine and studied it. She sighed.

"Mirror, mirror on the wall —" The words came haltingly to her mind and from her lips. She hadn't read them, she recalled. Daddy had said them, quoted them as he put it. But they too were lines from a book — "who is the fairest of —"

A picture of Mother sat upon the dresser and Mary considered this now. Looked for a long time at the slender, feminine neck. The golden skin, smooth and without blemish, without wrinkles and without age. The dark brown eyes and the thin tapers of eyebrows, the long black lashes, set evenly, so that each half of the face corresponded precisely. The half-parted-mouth, a violet tint against the gold, the white, white teeth, even, sparkling.

Mother. Beautiful, Transformed Mother. And back again to the mirror.

"— of them all. . . ."

The image of a rather chubby girl, without lines of rhythm or grace, without perfection. Splotchy skin full of little holes, puffs in the cheeks, red eruptions on the forehead. Perspiration, shapeless hair flowing onto shapeless shoulders down a shapeless body. Like all of them, before the Transformation.

Did they *all* look like this, before? Did Mother, even?

Mary thought hard, trying to remember exactly what Daddy and Grandpa had said, why they said the Transformation was a bad thing, and why she believed and agreed with them so strongly. It made little sense, but they were right. They *were* right! And one day, she would understand completely.

Mrs. Cuberle slammed the door angrily and Mary jumped to her feet. She hadn't forgotten about it. "The way you upset Dr. Hortel. He won't even see me anymore, and these traumas are getting horrible. I'll have to get that awful Dr. Wagoner."

"Sorry —"

Mrs. Cuberle sat on the couch and crossed her legs carefully.

"What in the world were you doing on the floor?"

"Trying to sleep."

"Now, I won't hear of it! You've got to stop it! You *know* you're not insane. Why should you want to do such a silly thing?"

"The books. And Daddy told me about it."

"And you mustn't read those terrible things."

"Why — is there a law against them?"

"Well, no, but people tired of books when the tapes came in. You know that. The house is full of tapes; anything you want."

Mary stuck out her lower lip.

"They're no fun. All about the Wars and the colonizations."

"And I suppose books are fun?"

"Yes. They are."

"And that's where you got this idiotic notion that you don't want the Transformation, isn't it? Of course it is. Well, we'll see to that!"

Mrs. Cuberle rose quickly and took the books from the corner and from the closet and filled her arms with them. She looked everywhere in the room and gathered the old rotten volumes.

These she carried from the room and threw into the elevator. A button guided the doors shut.

"I thought you'd do that," Mary said. "That's why I hid most of the good ones. Where you'll never find them."

Mrs. Cuberle put a satin handkerchief to her eyes and began to weep.

"Just look at you. Look. I don't know what I ever did to deserve this!"

"Deserve what, Mother? What am I doing that's so wrong?" Mary's mind rippled in a confused stream.

"What!" Mrs. Cuberle screamed, "*What!* Do you think I want people to point to you and say I'm the mother of an idiot? That's what they'll say, you'll see. Or," she looked up hopefully, "have you changed your mind?"

"No." The vague reasons, longing to be put into words.

"It doesn't hurt. They just take off a little skin and put some on and give you pills and electronic treatments and things like that. It doesn't take more than a week."

"No." The reason.

"Don't you want to be beautiful, like other people — like me? Look at your friend Shala, she's getting her Transformation next month. And *she's* almost pretty now."

"Mother, I don't care —"

"If it's the bones you're worried about, well, that doesn't hurt. They give you a shot and when you wake up, everything's molded right. Everything, to suit the personality."

"I don't care, I don't care."

"But *why?*"

"I like me the way I am." Almost — almost exactly. But not quite. Part of it, however. Part of what Daddy and Grandpa meant.

"But you're so ugly, dear! Like Dr. Hortel said. And Mr. Willmes, at the factory. He told some people he thought you were the ugliest girl he'd ever seen. Says he'll be thankful when you have your Transformation. And what if he hears of all this, what'll happen then?"

"Daddy said I was beautiful."

"Well really, dear. You *do* have eyes."

"Daddy said that real beauty is only skin deep. He said a lot of things like that and when I read the books I felt the same way. I guess I don't want to look like everybody else, that's all." No, that's not it. Not at all it.

"That man had too much to do with you. You'll notice that he had *his* Transformation, though!"

"But he was sorry. He told me that if he had it to do over again, he'd never do it. He said for me to be stronger than he was."

"Well, I won't have it. You're not going to get away with this, young lady. After all, I *am* your mother."

A bulb flickered in the bathroom and Mrs. Cuberle walked uncertainly to the cabinet. She took out a little cardboard box.

"Time for lunch."

Mary nodded. That was another thing the books talked about, which the tapes did not. Lunch seemed to be something special long ago, or at least different. The books talked of strange ways of putting a load of things into the mouth and chewing these things. Enjoying them. Strange and somehow wonderful.

"And you'd better get ready for work."

"Yes, Mother."

*T*he office was quiet and without shadows. The walls gave off a steady luminescence, distributed the light evenly upon all the desks and tables. And it was neither hot nor cold.

Mary held the ruler firmly and allowed the pen to travel down the metal edge effortlessly. The new black lines were small and accurate. She tipped her head, compared the notes beside her to the plan she was working on. She noticed the beautiful people looking at her more furtively than before, and she wondered about this as she made her lines.

A tall man rose from his desk in the rear of the office and walked down the aisle to Mary's table. He surveyed her work, allowing his eyes to travel cautiously from her face to the draft.

Mary looked around.

"Nice job," said the man.

"Thank you, Mr. Willmes."

"Dralich shouldn't have anything to complain about. That crane should hold the whole damn city."

"It's very good alloy, sir."

"Yeah. Say, kid, you got a minute?"

"Yes sir."

"Let's go into Mullinson's office."

The big handsome man led the way into a small cubby-hole of a room. He motioned to a chair and sat on the edge of one desk.

"Kid, I never was one to beat around the bush. Somebody called in little while ago, gave me some crazy story about you not wanting the Transformation."

Mary said "Oh." Daddy had said it would have to happen, some day. This must be what he meant.

"I would've told them they were way off the beam, but I wanted to talk to you first, get it straight."

"Well, sir, it's true. I don't. I want to stay this way."

The man looked at Mary and then coughed, embarrassedly.

"What the hell — excuse me, kid, but — I don't exactly get it. You, uh, you saw the psychiatrist?"

"Yes sir. I'm not insane. Dr. Hortel can tell you."

"I didn't mean anything like that. Well —" the man laughed nervously. "I don't know what to say. You're still a cub, but you do swell work. Lot of good results, lots of comments from the stations. But, Mr. Poole won't like it."

"I know. I know what you mean, Mr. Willmes. But nothing can change my mind. I want to stay this way and that's all there is to it."

"But — you'll get old before you're half through life."

Yes, she would. Old, like the Elders, wrinkled and brittle, unable to move right. Old. "It's hard to make you understand. But I don't see why it should make any difference."

"Don't go getting me wrong, now. It's not me, but, you know, I don't own Interplan. I just work here. Mr. Poole likes things running smooth and it's my job to carry it out. And soon as everybody finds out, things wouldn't run smooth. There'll be a big stink. The dames will start asking questions and talk."

"Will you accept my resignation, then, Mr. Willmes?"

"Sure you won't change your mind?"

"No sir. I decided that a long time ago. And I'm sorry now that I told Mother or anyone else. No sir, I won't change my mind."

"Well, I'm sorry, Mary. You been doing awful swell work. Couple of years you could be centralled on one of the asteroids, the way you been working. But if you should change your mind, there'll always be a job for you here."

"Thank you, sir."

"No hard feelings?"

"No hard feelings."

"Okay then. You've got till March. And between you and me, I hope by then you've decided the other way."

Mary walked back down the aisle, past the rows of desks. Past the men and women. The handsome, model men and the beautiful, perfect women, perfect, all perfect, all looking alike. Looking exactly alike.

She sat down again and took up her ruler and pen.

Mary stepped into the elevator and descended several hundred feet. At the Second Level she pressed a button and the elevator stopped. The doors opened with another button and the doors to her Unit with still another.

Mrs. Cuberle sat on the floor by the T-V, disconsolate and red-eyed. Her blond hair had come slightly askew and a few strands hung over her forehead. "You don't need to tell me. No one will hire you."

Mary sat beside her mother. "If you only hadn't told Mr. Willmes in the first place —"

"Well, I thought *he* could beat a little sense into you."

The sounds from the T-V grew louder. Mrs. Cuberle changed channels and finally turned it off.

"What did you do today, Mother?" Mary smiled.

"Do? What can I do, now? Nobody will even come over! I told you what would happen."

"Mother!"

"They say you should be in the Circuses."

Mary went into another room. Mrs. Cuberle followed. "How are we going to live? Where does the money come from now? Just because you're stubborn on this crazy idea. Crazy crazy crazy! Can I support both of us? They'll be firing *me*, next!"

"Why is this happening?"

"Because of you, that's why. Nobody else on this planet has ever refused the Transformation. But you turn it down. You *want* to be ugly!"

Mary put her arms about her mother's shoulders. "I wish I could explain, I've tried so hard to. It isn't that I want to bother anyone, or that Daddy wanted me to. I just don't want the Transformation."

Mrs. Cuberle reached into the pockets of her blouse and got a purple pill. She swallowed the pill. When the letter dropped from the chute, Mrs. Cuberle ran to snatch it up. She read it once, silently, then smiled.

"Oh, I was afraid they wouldn't answer. But we'll see about this *now!*"

She gave the letter to Mary.

Mrs. Zena Cuberle
Unit 451 D
Levels II & III
City
Dear Madam:

In re your letter of Dec 3 36. We have carefully examined your complaint and consider that it requires stringent measures. Quite frankly, the possibility of such a complaint has never occurred to this Dept. and we therefore cannot make positive directives at the moment.

However, due to the unusual qualities of the matter, we have arranged an audience at Centraldome, Eighth Level, Sixteenth Unit, Jan 3 37, 23 sharp. Dr. Elph Hortel has been instructed to attend. You will bring the subject in question.

Yrs,
Dept F

Mary let the paper flutter to the floor. She walked quietly to the elevator and set it for Level III. When the elevator stopped, she ran from it, crying, into her room.

She thought and remembered and tried to sort out and put together. Daddy had said it, Grandpa had, the books did. Yes, the books did.

She read until her eyes burned and her eyes burned until she could read no more. Then Mary went to sleep, softly and without realizing it, for the first time.

But the sleep was not peaceful.

"*L*adies and gentlemen," said the young-looking, well groomed man, "this problem does not resolve easily. Dr. Hortel here, testifies that Mary Cuberle is definitely not insane. Drs. Monagh, Prinn and Fedders all verify this judgment. Dr. Prinn asserts that the human organism is no longer so constructed as to create and sustain such an attitude through deliberate falsehood. Further, there is positively nothing in the structure of Mary Cuberle which might suggest difficulties in Transformation. There is evidence for all these statements. And yet we are faced with this refusal. What, may I ask, is to be done?"

Mary looked at a metal table.

"We have been in session far too long, holding up far too many other pressing contingencies. The trouble on Mercury, for example. We'll *have* to straighten that out, somehow."

Throughout the rows of beautiful people, the mumbling increased. Mrs. Cuberle sat nervously, tapping her shoe and running a comb through her hair.

"Mary Cuberle, you have been given innumerable chances to reconsider, you know."

Mary said, "I know. But I don't want to."

The beautiful people looked at Mary and laughed. Some shook their heads.

The man threw up his hands. "Little girl, can you realize what an issue you have caused? The unrest, the wasted time? Do you fully understand what you have done? Intergalactic questions hang fire while you sit there saying the same thing over and over. Doesn't the happiness of your Mother mean anything to you?"

A slender, supple woman in a back row cried, "We want action. *Do* something!"

The man in the high stool raised his hand. "None of that, now. We must conform, even though the question is out of the ordinary." He leafed through a number of papers on his desk, leaned down and whispered into the ear of a strong blond man. Then he turned to Mary again. "Child, for the last time. Do you reconsider? Will you accept the Transformation?"

"No."

The man shrugged his shoulders. "Very well, then. I have here a petition, signed by two thousand individuals and representing all the Stations of Earth. They have been made aware of all the facts and have submitted the petition voluntarily. It's all so unusual and I'd hoped we wouldn't have to — but the petition urges drastic measures."

The mumbling rose.

"The petition urges that you shall, upon final refusal, be forced by law to accept the Transformation. And that an act of legislature shall make this universal and binding in the future."

Mary's eyes were open, wide. She stood and paused before speaking.

"Why?" she asked, loudly.

The man passed a hand through his hair.

Another voice from the crowd, "Seems to be a lot of questions unanswered here."

And another, "Sign the petition, Senator!"

All the voices, "Sign it, sign it!"

"But why?" Mary began to cry. The voices stilled for a moment.

"Because — Because —"

"If you'd only tell me that. Tell me!"

"Why, it simply isn't being done, that's all. The greatest gift of all, and what if others should get the same idea? What would happen to us then, little girl? We'd be right back to the ugly, thin, fat, unhealthy-looking race we were ages ago! There can't be any exceptions."

"Maybe they didn't consider themselves so ugly."

The mumbling began anew.

"That isn't the point," cried the man. "You *must* conform!"

And the voices cried "Yes" loudly until the man took up a pen and signed the papers on his desk.

Cheers, applause, shouts.

Mrs. Cuberle patted Mary on the top of her head.

"There, now!" she said, happily, "Everything will be all right now. You'll see, Mary."

*T*he Transformation Parlor Covered the entire Level, sprawling with its departments. It was always filled and there was nothing to sign and no money to pay and people were always waiting in line.

But today the people stood aside. And there were still more, looking in through doors, TV cameras placed throughout the tape machines in every corner. It was filled, but not bustling as usual.

Mary walked past the people, Mother and the men in back of her, following. She looked at the people. The people were beautiful, perfect, without a single flaw.

All the beautiful people. All the ugly people, staring out from bodies that were not theirs. Walking on legs that had been made for them, laughing with manufactured voices, gesturing with shaped and fashioned arms.

Mary walked slowly, despite the prodding. In her eyes, in *her* eyes, was a mounting confusion; a wide, wide wonderment.

The reason was becoming less vague; the fuzzed edges were falling away now. Through all the horrible months and all the horrible moments, the edges fell away. Now it was almost clear.

She looked down at her own body, then at the walls which reflected it. Flesh of her flesh, bone of her bone, all hers, made by no one, built by herself or someone she did not know. Uneven kneecaps, making two grinning cherubs when they bent, and the old familiar rubbing together of fat inner thighs. Fat, unshapely, unsystematic Mary. But *Mary*.

Of course. Of course! This *was* what Daddy meant, what Grandpa and the books meant. What *they* would know if they would read the books or hear the words, the good, reasonable words, the words that signified more, much more, than any of this.

The understanding heaped up with each step.

"Where *are* these people?" Mary asked half to herself. "What has happened to *them* and don't they miss *themselves*, these manufactured things?"

She stopped, suddenly.

"Yes! That *is* the reason. They have all forgotten themselves!"

A curvacious woman stepped forward and took Mary's hand. The woman's skin was tinted dark. Chipped and sculptured bone into slender rhythmic lines, electrically created carriage, stance, made, turned out.

"All right, young lady. We will begin."

They guided Mary to a large, curved leather seat.

From the top of a long silver pole a machine lowered itself. Tiny bulbs glowed to life and cells began to click. The people stared. Slowly a picture formed upon the screen in the machine. Bulbs directed at Mary, then redirected into the machine. Wheels turning, buttons ticking.

The picture was completed.

"Would you like to see it?"

Mary closed her eyes, tight.

"It's really very nice." The woman turned to the crowd. "Oh yes, there's a great deal to be salvaged; you'd be surprised. A great deal. We'll keep the nose and I don't believe the elbows will have to be altered at all."

Mrs. Cuberle looked at Mary and smiled. "Now, it isn't so bad as you thought, is it?" she said.

The beautiful people looked. Cameras turned, tapes wound.

"You'll have to excuse us now. Only the machines allowed."

Only the machines.

The people filed out.

Mary saw the rooms in the mirror. Saw things in the rooms, the faces and bodies that had been left; the woman and the machines and the old young men standing about, adjusting, readying.

Then she looked at the picture in the screen.

And screamed.

A woman of medium height stared back at her. A woman with a curved body and thin legs; silver hair, pompadoured, cut short; full sensuous lips, small breasts, flat stomach, unblemished skin.

A strange, strange woman no one had ever seen before.

The nurse began to take Mary's clothes off.

"Geoff," the woman said, "come look at this, will you. Not one so bad in years. Amazing that we can keep anything at all."

The handsome man put his hands in his pockets.

"Pretty bad, all right."

"Be still, child, stop making those noises. You know perfectly well nothing is going to hurt."

"But — what will you do with me?"

"That was all explained to you."

"No, no, with *me, me!*"

"Oh, you mean the castoffs. The usual. I don't know exactly. Somebody takes care of it."

"I want me!" Mary cried. "Not that!" She pointed at the screen.

*H*er chair was wheeled into a semi-dark room. She was naked now, and the men lifted her to a table. The surface was like glass, black, filmed. A big machine hung above.

Straps. Clamps pulling, stretching limbs apart. The screen with the picture brought in. The men and the woman, more women now. Dr. Hortel in a corner, sitting with his legs crossed, shaking his head.

Mary began to cry above the hum of the mechanical things.

"Shhh. My gracious, such a racket! Just think about your job waiting for you, and all the friends you'll have and how nice everything will be. No more trouble now."

The big machine hurtling downward.

"Where will I find *me?*" Mary screamed, "when it's all over?"

A long needle slid into rough flesh and the beautiful people gathered around the table.

They turned on the big machine.

THE END

www.ingramcontent.com/pod-product-compliance
Lightning Source LLC
Chambersburg PA
CBHW031905170626
46807CB00004B/1914